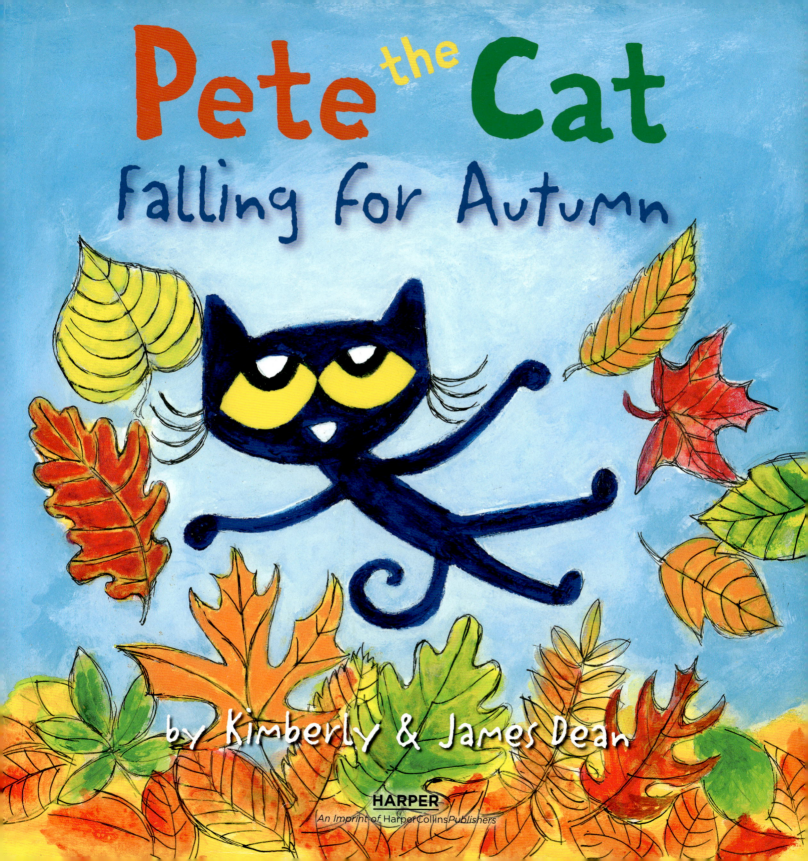

Pete the Cat
Falling for Autumn

by Kimberly & James Dean

HARPER

An Imprint of HarperCollinsPublishers

Pete the Cat: Falling for Autumn
Text copyright © 2020 by James Dean and Kimberly Dean
Art copyright © 2020 by James Dean
Pete the Cat is a registered trademark of Pete the Cat, LLC.
All rights reserved. Manufactured in China.
No part of this book may be used or reproduced in any manner whatsoever without written
permission except in the case of brief quotations embodied in critical articles and reviews.
For information address HarperCollins Children's Books, a division of HarperCollins Publishers,
195 Broadway, New York, NY 10007.
www.harpercollinschildrens.com

ISBN 978-0-06-286848-0

The artist used pen and ink, with watercolor and acrylic paint,
on 300lb hot press paper to create the illustrations for this book.
Book Designed by Jeanne L. Hogle
20 21 22 23 24 SCP 10 9 8 7 6 5 4 3 2 1
❖
First Edition

It is the first day of fall, and Pete the Cat is feeling blue.

"I like summer better," he says. "In summer, I can swim and surf and play at the beach."

"Maybe you just need to remind yourself of all the things you love about autumn," Mom suggests.

"Hmm," Pete says. "I'll try . . ."

Pete finds Grandma in the kitchen. She's baking delicious pumpkin pies. The whole house smells sweet and spicy.

Pete loves helping Grandma bake pumpkin pie, but he loves helping eat it even more!

After the baking is done, Pete picks a squat orange pumpkin from the counter and slips it into his backpack as a souvenir.

Next Pete heads to the town corn maze. Pete and his friends wander through the long twisty paths made of tall cornstalks.

The best part of the corn maze is getting lost and having to start over again!

Next Pete goes to the hayride at the park. Pete, Bob, Mom, Dad, and Grandpa all pile into a wagon filled with hay. They go on a bumpy wagon ride around the park.

"Woo-hoo!" Pete shouts.

When they're done, Pete chooses a little ball
of leftover yarn and places it inside his backpack.

Then Pete visits Grandpa, who is knitting on the porch. Grandpa helps Pete use the knitting needles to knit the yarn into cool patterns.

Together, Pete and Grandpa make a long cozy scarf for Pete to wear.

As he leaves, Pete plucks
a golden corncob from the
maze and places it inside his
backpack.

At the end of the ride, Pete grabs a
handful of sweet-smelling hay from the
wagon and stuffs it into his backpack.

Pete heads over to the apple orchard, where he and Callie go apple picking.

They eat sweet apple donuts and drink hot apple cider and fill their buckets with apples of all different shapes and sizes.

Before he leaves, Pete chooses a round red apple and drops it into his backpack.

Next Pete stops by the park. He plays touch football
with Bob and their friends. Pete scores a touchdown,
and everyone cheers!

After the game, Pete grabs Bob's football and stuffs it into his backpack. It barely fits!

"Bob won't mind if I borrow this."
Pete says.

Finally, Pete heads back home. But he stops in his front yard, which is covered in bright leaves falling from the trees.

Pete helps his dad rake the leaves into big colorful mounds. Then Pete runs and jumps into all the leaf piles.

After he's done jumping, Pete picks a bunch of red and gold and orange leaves and stuffs them into his backpack.

Pete's backpack is bursting with fall souvenirs.
He can't wait to show Mom!
"I LOVE autumn!" Pete says.

"Wonderful!" says Mom. "You know . . . these
would make great decorations for Thanksgiving."

So Pete helps Mom fill a basket with all his mementos.
They place the basket at the center of the table.
"You did a great job, Pete!" says Mom.
"It's beautiful!" says Dad.

"Is that my football?" asks Bob.
Just then, the doorbell rings.

The Thanksgiving guests are here! All of Pete's family and friends gather around the dining room table. They tell stories and laugh at jokes while they eat. Everyone is having a great time.

Pete looks around the table and smiles. He loves lots of things about autumn, but Pete knows what he loves most all year long . . .

. . . his family and friends.

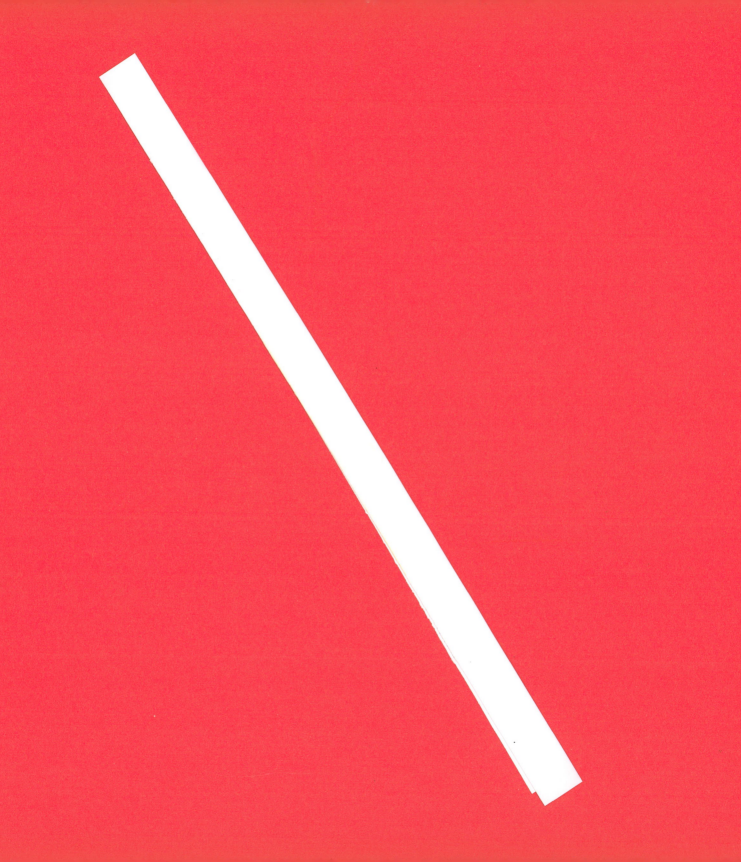